# Natural Partners

Alan Trussell-Cullen

Australia • Brazil • Japan • Korea • Mexico • Singapore • Spain • United Kingdom • United States

Natural Partners

Fast Forward
Orange Level 15

Text: Alan Trussell-Cullen
Editor: Cameron Macintosh
Design: Stella Vassiliou
Series design: James Lowe
Production controller: Emma Hayes
Photo research: Gillian Cardinal
Audio recordings: Juliet Hill, Picture Start
Spoken by: Matthew King and Abbe Holmes
Reprint: Jennifer Foo

Acknowledgements
The author and publisher would like to acknowledge permission to reproduce material from the following sources: Photographs by Getty Images/Stone, p 4/ National Geographic, p 5; FLPA/Toney Whittaker, p 8/ Peter Davey, p 9/ Nigel Cattlin, p 21; Bruce Coleman/Phillip Colla, p 16; Auscape International/Becca Saunders, pp 18-19; Photolibrary.com/Pacific Stock, front cover, pp 1, 14-15/ Mauritius Die Bildagentur Gmbh, back cover, p 23/ Oxford Scientific Films, pp 12-13, 20 bottom/ Alamy/F. Jack Jackson, p 17/ Science Photo Library, p 20 top/ Botanica, p 22; Warren Photographic, pp 3, 6-7; Marine Themes, pp 10-11.



ISBN 978 0 17 012605 2
ISBN 978 0 17 012597 0 (set)

Cengage Learning Australia
Level 7, 80 Dorcas Street
South Melbourne, Victoria Australia 3205
Phone: 1300 790 853

Cengage Learning New Zealand
Unit 4B Rosedale Office Park
331 Rosedale Road, Albany, North Shore NZ 0632
Phone: 0508 635 766

For learning solutions, visit cengage.com.au

Printed in Australia by Ligare Pty Ltd
7 8 9 10 11 12 13 21 20 19 18 17

Evaluated in independent research by staff from the Department of Language, Literacy and Arts Education at the University of Melbourne.

# Natural Partners

Alan Trussell-Cullen

## Contents

Chapter 1

# NATURAL PARTNERS

**Natural** partners are animals or plants that live or work together, to help themselves and each other.

The tickbird and the rhinoceros are natural partners. The tickbird looks for ticks while riding on the rhinoceros's back.

This is good for the rhinoceros because it stays **healthy** without the ticks. It's also good for the tickbird because it gets an easy meal.

When there is danger, the tickbird flies into the air, screaming a warning to the rhinoceros.

The crocodile also has a bird as a natural partner. The crocodile opens its mouth so that the bird can get right inside.

The bird gives the crocodile's mouth and teeth a really good clean.
The bird gets a really good feed by cleaning the crocodile's mouth.

The badger also has a bird as a natural partner.

Both this bird and the badger eat honey.
The bird flies around looking for a bee nest.
When it finds one, it calls out to the badger.

The bees do not harm the badger,
so the badger pulls the nest to bits to get the honey.



Running Words 180

The bird stays around waiting for any honey that the badger drops.

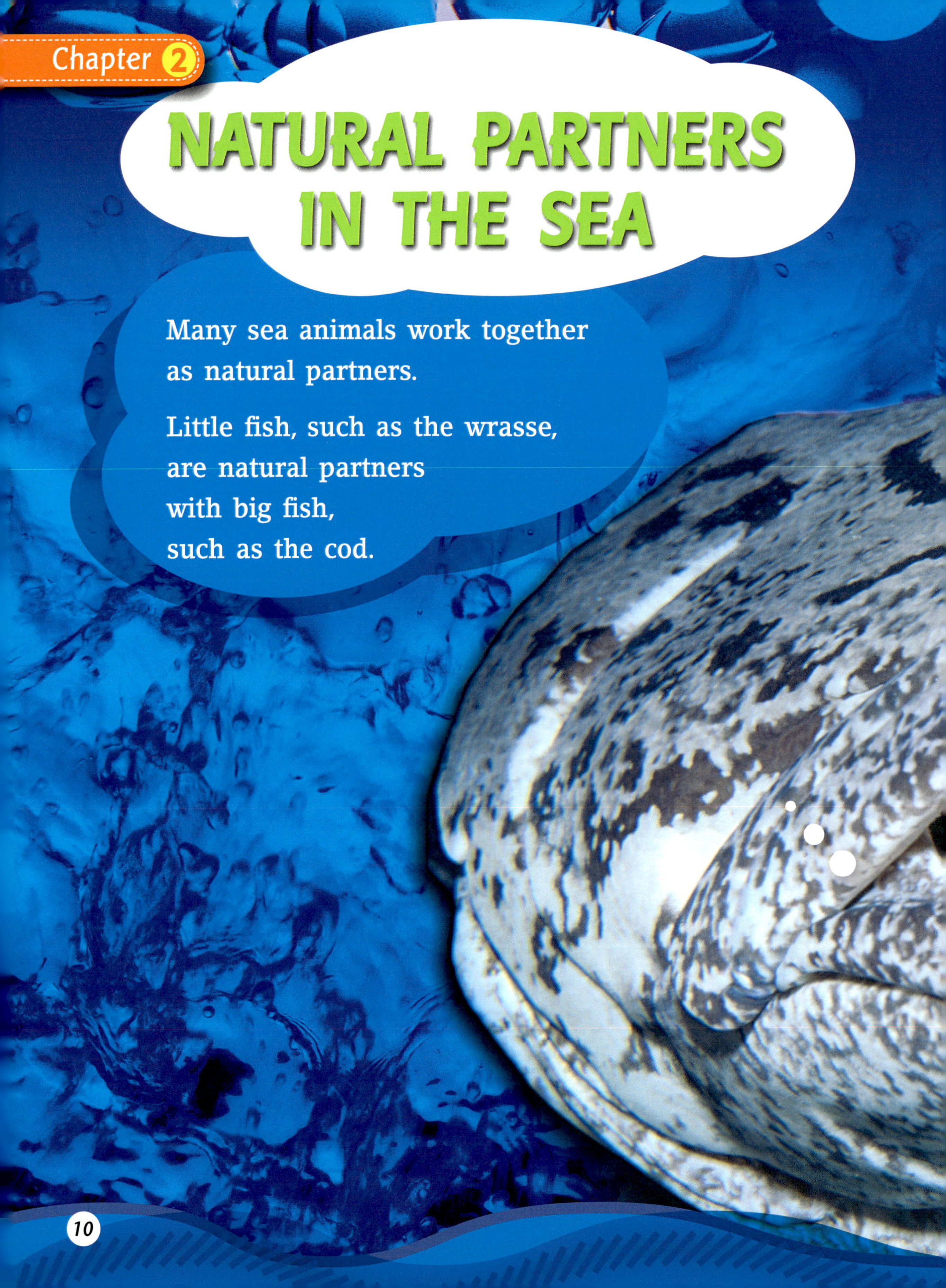

Chapter 2

# NATURAL PARTNERS IN THE SEA

Many sea animals work together as natural partners.

Little fish, such as the wrasse, are natural partners with big fish, such as the cod.

The wrasse cleans the cod –
even inside its mouth.
The cod gets a good clean,
and the wrasse gets a good feed.

The hermit crab and the anemone are also natural partners.
Anemones grow on the hermit crab's shell.
Anemones have tentacles that sting,
so they **protect** the hermit crab from its enemies.

The anemones then get to catch food as the crab moves around.

Anemones are also natural partners with clownfish. The anemone's stings don't hurt clownfish, so clownfish can live with them.

However, the anemone stings the clownfish's enemies, which helps to protect the clownfish.

The clownfish helps the anemone by dropping scraps of food for it to eat.

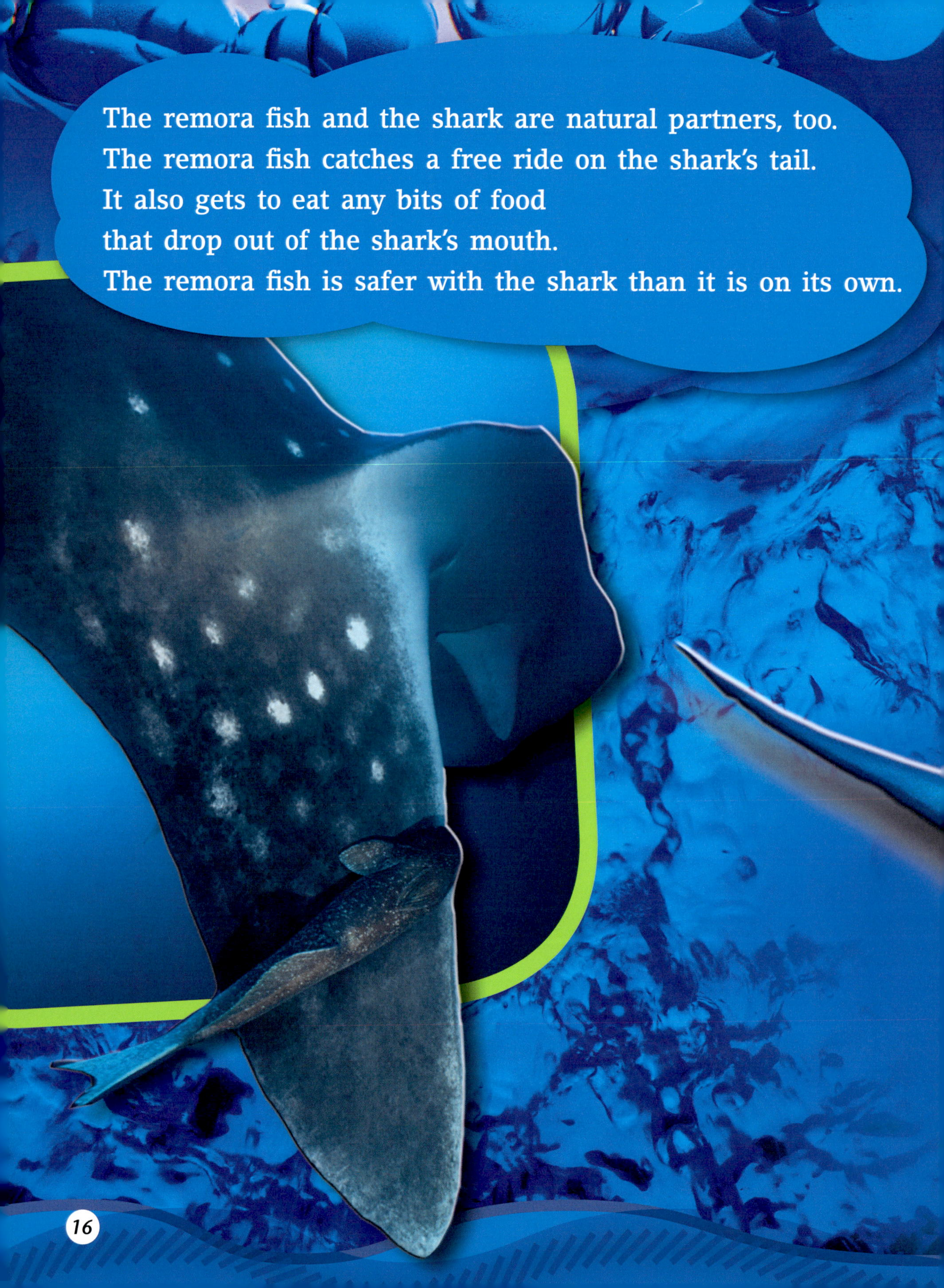

The remora fish and the shark are natural partners, too.
The remora fish catches a free ride on the shark's tail.
It also gets to eat any bits of food
that drop out of the shark's mouth.
The remora fish is safer with the shark than it is on its own.

The remora fish removes **parasites** from the shark's skin, as the shark swims along.
This helps keep the shark healthy.

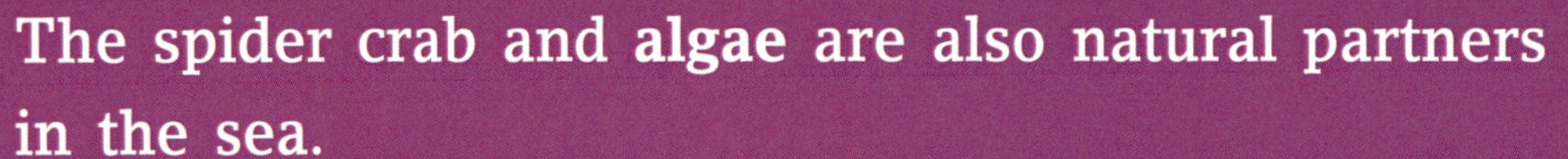

The spider crab and **algae** are also natural partners in the sea.

The spider crab lives on the sea floor.
Algae live on the spider crab's back,
making the spider crab look like part of the sea floor.
This makes it hard for the spider crab's enemies to see it.

The algae get a good place to live, and the crab has a good camouflage.

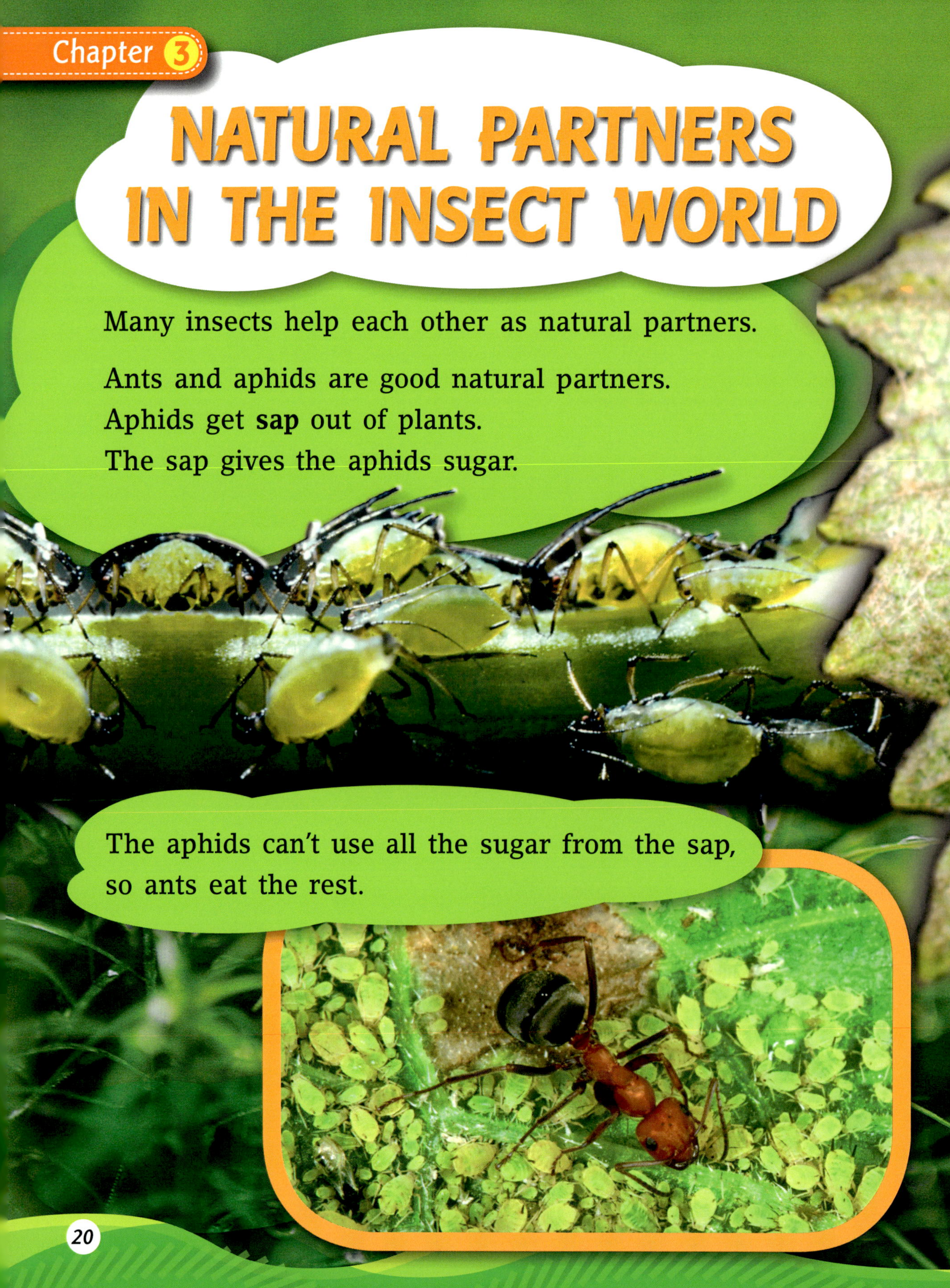

Chapter 3

# NATURAL PARTNERS IN THE INSECT WORLD

Many insects help each other as natural partners.

Ants and aphids are good natural partners.
Aphids get **sap** out of plants.
The sap gives the aphids sugar.

The aphids can't use all the sugar from the sap, so ants eat the rest.

While the aphids help the ants by giving them food, the ants protect the aphids by attacking their enemies.

Bees and many flowering plants are natural partners.

Bees use **nectar** to make honey.
They get their nectar from flowers.
As bees fly from flower to flower,
they also take **pollen** from one flower to another.
This helps the flowering plant grow seeds,
which then grow into new plants.

## Glossary

**algae** tiny plants that live in the water

**healthy** well, in good health

**natural** what happens in nature

**nectar** a sweet liquid made by plants, and used by bees to make honey

**parasites** plants or animals that live off other living things

**pollen** small grains in flowers that help other flowers to make seeds

**protect** keep safe

**sap** the liquid found inside plants

## Index